About the author

GW00854624

David Fuller is an FA-qu:
and currently coaches a y
in Brighton. He has worked as a journalist for
more than a decade, during which time he has
written for numerous publications on a variety of
different subjects. David lives in Newhaven, East
Sussex with his wife, two sons and cat Merry.

Other books by David Fuller

Alfie Jones and a Change of Fortune
Alfie Jones and a Test of Character
Alfie Jones and the Missing Link
Alfie Jones and an Uncertain Future
Alfie Jones and the Big Decision

RDF Publishing
3 Courtlands Mews, Church Hill, Newhaven,
East Sussex,
BN9 9LU

A Footballer's Christmas Carol
A RDF Publishing book

First published in Great Britain by RDF Publishing in 2016
Available on Kindle since 2013
Printed and bound in Great Britain by Clays Ltd,
St Ives plc
1

ISBN 978-0-9570339-5-5

For more exclusive Alfie Jones content, visit:
www.alfie-jones.co.uk

A
FOOTBALLER'S
CHRISTMAS
CAROL

DAVID FULLER

www.alfie-jones.co.uk

Rich boy

Jacob Anderson is rich. Very rich indeed.

Of that there is absolutely no doubt.

None whatsoever.

Imagine the largest amount of money you can. Times it by two. Or three. Or four. Maybe even by ten.

That's how rich Jacob Anderson is.

Filthy, stinking rich.

And he's not shy about letting everyone know it.

One day you might see him leaving his house – well, his luxury seven-bedroom, mock-Tudor country mansion – in a brand new Mercedes-Benz. The next he'll be swanning around town in the latest Range Rover Sport.

Jacob Anderson, you see, has a different car for every single day of the week.

Not that he's allowed to drive any of them, mind you. Oh no. He's banned from driving. He got caught going over 200 miles per hour on a motorway.

Twice.

Instead, his cars are driven for him by his personal assistant, Norris Sculley. Well, I say personal assistant. A more accurate description would be 'personal slave'.

Put simply, Norris does anything and everything that Jacob asks – or rather tells – him to. He drives Jacob wherever he wants to go. Washes his clothes. Cleans his house, Makes sure he's always where he's supposed to be when he's supposed to be there. He even has to text people when Jacob can't be bothered to pick up his 24-carat gold iphone. Which is often.

Yet Norris hasn't always been Jacob's personal 'assistant'.

In fact, up until five years ago they were best friends. Had been for years. Ever since first meeting at infant school.

But then something happened to Jacob. Something that made him so very rich and, eventually, turned him into the far from pleasant person he is today.

He became a professional footballer.

The reluctant assistant

At first Jacob was only too keen to share his good fortune with his best friend.

Shortly after signing his first professional contract with Premier League Westpool Athletic, he decided to employ Norris as his agent.

While Norris hadn't been particularly athletic at school, he had always been clever. And very, very good at maths. Jacob believed that Norris would be the ideal person to handle his finances.

And, for a while, he was right.

Norris soon helped Jacob become rich. Not filthy, stinking rich, like he is now. But extremely well off nevertheless.

However, three years into his professional football career, Jacob still wasn't earning as much money as some of his lesser talented teammates. This was a situation that he did not think was at all fair.

By this point, Jacob had become a firm favourite with the Westpool fans. Many football experts were starting to suggest that he had the potential to become the club's best ever player. Even better

than the legendary Timothy Marley –
Athletic's all time leading goal scorer.

As interest from other top clubs
started to materialise, Westpool became
increasingly desperate to keep hold of
their star player. Something that Jacob
was only too aware of. He began ordering
Norris to hold the club's directors to
ransom.

He commanded his friend to get him
as much money as possible. He even
told Norris he would join a rival team if
Westpool didn't give him the stupendous
wages he – and many of the club's fans –
believed he was worth.

Not being the kind of man who enjoys
any sort of confrontation, Norris refused
to enter into such negotiations. Instead
he tried to make his friend see the error
of his ways.

He failed miserably.

Jacob couldn't believe that Norris would
not do exactly as he was being asked –
well, ordered – and sacked him as his
agent immediately.

However, when, some months later,
Jacob discovered his former friend had
failed to find another job, he offered
Norris the chance to become his personal
assistant. But only if Norris would agree

to do absolutely anything that was asked of him.

Norris really hadn't wanted to accept the offer. But he had a mortgage to pay and a family to feed, so ultimately he had no option but to swallow his pride and return to work for his one-time best buddy.

The lucky pants

Since becoming Jacob's personal assistant almost five years ago, Norris had become used to performing all manner of humiliating tasks. He was once ordered to paint a garden wall using only a toothbrush!

But nothing could have prepared him for what he currently found himself doing.

Namely, walking up and down his local high street while waving a stick with a pair of dark blue pants attached to the top, high above his head.

Being Christmas Eve, and with the street chock-full of people doing some last minute shopping, there were far more shoppers around than usual. Most of whom were finding great humour in poor Norris's humiliation.

When Jacob had told Norris what he'd wanted him to do earlier that afternoon, Norris had foolishly assumed that the footballer was joking.

He quickly realised he wasn't.

"They're my lucky pants," Jacob had explained, as innocently as possible. "I need them to be dry in time for my match on Boxing Day."

"They'll dry on the radiator in plenty of time. Or I could just put them in the tumble dryer," Norris had pleaded, in a quite reasonable manner.

"Don't argue with me," Jacob roared at his assistant. "They have to be dried this way. It's the only way they'll bring me any luck. I haven't scored a goal for three games when they've been dried the 'normal' way, so we're going to try this. I take it you do want your Christmas bonus this year?"

Norris was about to plead his case some more, but talk of a Christmas bonus soon convinced him to stop and begrudgingly accept his task.

When he had first been his agent many years earlier, Jacob had been more than generous when it came to Christmas bonuses. He had once given Norris a car from his sizable fleet. He still drove that car now; an eight-year-old Porsche Cayenne.

Finally, after the requested three hours of parading up and down the high street while waving the footballer's pants around like a flag, Norris got back into the car that he and Jacob had arrived in a few hours earlier – an Audi R8.

"There you go," said Norris handing the pants to Jacob, who had been watching his assistant's performance from behind the Audi's blacked out windows. "Nice and dry. You're bound to score on Boxing Day now," he added, sarcastically.

"Whatever," said Jacob, sounding bored. He nonchalantly tossed the pants onto the back seat of the car, without so much as even glancing at them.

The truth was that Jacob had never worn those blue pants before in his life. He probably never would. He just thought it would be funny to send Norris out into the High Street waving them around on a stick.

He was right. It had been funny.

Well, for everyone except for Norris, that is.

Decisions, Decisions

Not all that surprisingly, Norris felt miserable as he drove Jacob back to his country mansion.

No matter how hard he tried, he couldn't shake from his mind the memory of all the Christmas shoppers laughing at him.

Not that Jacob seemed to notice his assistant's discontent. Throughout the entirety of their 20-minute drive home, Jacob did nothing but talk about what car he should buy himself as a Christmas treat.

He couldn't make up his mind between a convertible Lamborghini or an Aston Martin DB9 Coupe. In the end he decided he'd just get both.

"I've got a mate who reckons he can get hold of a brand new DB9 for £125,000 and a convertible Lamborghini for around £250,000," he reasoned aloud. "I mean, that's a bargain, innit? Can't turn down offers like that! I earn much more than that in a month. And I've got another sponsorship deal on the table that should be worth a few more million. I might even take a look at the new Maserati. That looks like a pretty tasty motor."

Norris tuned out as Jacob continued waffling on about how much money he earned and came up with increasingly ludicrous ways of how he should spend it.

If the footballer was only a quarter as generous when it came to paying his staff as he was with his own self indulgences, then maybe Norris would have been able to afford a decent Christmas meal for the following day. Instead he was once again being forced to rely on supermarket offers and hand-outs from friends.

Still, maybe his Christmas bonus would make up for his miniscule pay packet.

Norris certainly hoped so.

Not a fan of fans

Norris slowed the car as they approached the huge golden gates which stood at the entrance to Jacob's mansion.

Jacob was in the middle of trying to decide which colours his soon-to-be new cars should be when, through the windscreen, he spotted something that made him shudder.

"Oh no," he sighed loudly. "What do they want now?"

While Jacob loved most of the rewards that came with being a professional footballer – namely the humongous wads of cash – there were some things he hated. One was training. He didn't see why he should have to bother with this when his manager already knew that he was amazing. The thing he despised more than anything about being footballer, though, were the fans.

He could tolerate them on match days, when they were singing his name in the stands a safe distance away from him. He absolutely loved seeing people staring gog-eyed at him as he drove – or more accurately was driven – past them in one of his many flashy cars.

But he couldn't bear being approached by them in the street. Or at a restaurant. Or outside Westpool's stadium.

Anywhere.

Least of all outside his house.

Therefore, upon seeing two young boys dressed in full Westpool kits standing outside his mansion's magnificent golden gates, with a lady he took to be their mother, his mood considerably darkened.

"I don't suppose you could just run them over?" Jacob asked Norris, more in hope than expectation.

"No I can't," said Norris, sounding genuinely horrified. There were some things that even Norris drew the line at doing for Jacob.

"Relax. I'm just joking," Jacob lied. "Right, I've got an idea, innit," he said, after a moment's thought. "I'll pretend to be asleep while you go and speak to them. Tell them that I'm under team orders to sleep at this exact time every single day and that I'll get dropped if I'm found to be awake. That'll get rid of 'em," Jacob smiled, clearly delighted with what he considered to be a plan of complete and utter genius.

"Couldn't you just sign an autograph for them? It would only take you a minute or two," suggested the footballer's assistant.

Jacob sighed loudly again. "Why should I?" he whined. "Just because I'm a supremely talented individual who brings pleasure to thousands of people each and every week, those, those... fans seem to think it's okay to stop me in public places demanding I sign pieces of paper for them. Well I won't do it. It's not fair."

Norris rolled his eyes and then got out of the car. He had tried reasoning with Jacob before about signing autographs. Countless times, he had explained to him

that without the supporters he wouldn't
be paid the extortionate amounts he was
to do a job that millions dream of doing.

Jacob hadn't listened then and Norris
knew another attempt to change his mind
would just be a waste of time.

"Is that him?" asked the unimpressed
sounding woman as Norris approached.
"He's a lot scrawnier than I thought
he would be! He looks more like an
accountant than a footballer."

"Don't be stupid, Mum," said one of the
identical looking young boys. "Course
that isn't him. That's probably just his
butler or something."

Norris bristled at being called a
butler. Mainly because the young boy's
description was sadly spot on.

"I'm afraid Jacob's asleep at the
moment," explained Norris, just as the
footballer let out a hugely unconvincing
fake snore. "He has to sleep at this
time every single day," he continued,
trying to ignore the increasingly loud
and progressively unconvincing snores
coming from the direction of the car.
"Management orders, I'm afraid."

"But we've travelled for miles and
waited in the cold for three hours just to
see him," begged the woman. "I've saved

up all year to buy my two boys the latest Westpool kits. It's their Birthday today and as I can't afford a Christmas present for them as well as a Birthday present, I said we'd see if we could get Jacob Anderson to sign their kit. He's their favourite player. They love him."

The two boys nodded earnestly and gave Norris their best puppy dog eyes.

Norris looked pleadingly in the direction of the car. He couldn't see Jacob because of the Audi's blacked out windows but he knew full well that Jacob could see him.

Jacob's only response was to snore even louder.

"I'm really sorry. There's nothing I can do," said Norris, hoping he sounded as wretched as he felt.

The two boys started to sob loudly.

"Well Merry Christmas to you, too," the mother shouted angrily. She gently ushered the two boys away from the golden gates, and started walking along the country lane in the opposite direction from where Norris had just driven. Norris couldn't see a car anywhere and had to wonder how far they had walked. The nearest bus stop was more than five miles away, while the closest train station was even further.

Norris climbed back into the car feeling awful. He was amazed to find that Jacob was in fits of laughter.

"Well done Norris," he said. "A job well done, innit," he added, giving his assistant a friendly wink.

The man den

Once safely inside the house, Jacob quickly made his way towards his favourite room. His 'man den'.

Comprising two snooker tables, a pool table, a table tennis table, countless dart boards, every single games console you can imagine and a ten-pin bowling alley, Jacob's man den is simply huge.

However, what really makes the room so special is the television. With a screen measuring over five-metres wide, builders had had to knock down numerous walls just to get it inside the house.

The television cost Jacob a little over £400,000 and it had cost almost half that amount again to carry out the renovation work needed to get the giant screen into the mansion.

But Jacob firmly believed it was worth

every single penny. He loved that TV. Almost as much as he loved his cars.

"Hello my little beauty," said Jacob, as if to talking to a tiny baby. The footballer walked over to the television and affectionately patted its side. Suddenly a look of pure panic swept across his face.

"NORRIS," he screamed at the top of his voice. He sounded truly terrified. "NORRIS. GET. HERE. NOW."

Norris hurried into the room as fast as he could. He couldn't remember ever having heard his boss sound so panicked. "Jacob, what is it? What's wrong?" He was surprised at how concerned he felt about his former friend.

"Where's the remote control? I can't see it anywhere."

A look of pure disbelief swept across Norris's face. Jacob still looked utterly petrified. "It's there," he said, pointing towards a diamond encrusted coffee table on which the remote was sat.

The table was placed little more than two feet away from where Jacob was standing.

"Oh thank goodness for that," replied a clearly relieved Jacob. The footballer stooped down, picked up the remote control and then tossed it to the unsuspecting Norris, who just about managed to catch it. "Turn it on and put the sports news on for me," he demanded.

"Could you not have done it? You had the remote in your hand."

Jacob shot Norris an angry look. "What's the point of having you here if I have to turn on my own TV? What if I sprain a finger? You really are a selfish little so-and-so sometimes, innit."

Norris looked dumbfounded, but managed to stop himself from saying anything further. It was nearly time for him to go home for the day.

More importantly, it was nearly time for his Christmas bonus.

The TV came on and Norris, as instructed, flicked over to the 24-hour sports news channel.

"And after a short break we've got a real Christmas treat coming up for you as we'll be joined in the studio by a real legend of the game," announced the pretty, young female presenter.

"That's right, Westpool Athletic's all-time leading goal scorer, Timothy Marley, will be here to discuss the upcoming festive football fixtures, so stay tuned," added the woman's older, not so attractive, male colleague.

"Oh no!" Jacob grumbled loudly. "What has that old buffoon got to say for himself now?"

Marley's record

Even though he had retired from playing football more than 15 years ago, Timothy Marley was still much loved by Westpool Athletic's fans.

Hardly surprising really. A return of 177 league goals in 233 games would make him a legend at any club.

Yet anyone with only a passing interest in football was of the opinion that it wouldn't be too long before Jacob beat Marley's record. He had already scored 151 goals in just 205 games. And at the age of 26 he still had plenty of time to surpass Marley's haul.

It was something that Jacob was desperate to do. And the sooner he could do it the better.

When he was a young boy, Jacob had dreamed long and hard about how great it would feel to score the winning goal in an FA Cup final. Now, he considered that dream to be nothing more than childish foolishness. He no longer cared about winning trophies – although he had to admit the win bonuses that came with them were nice.

In years to come, Jacob truly believed that while people may remember that Westpool had won a trophy, they wouldn't necessarily remember anything about the players that had played for the team.

Jacob couldn't even remember who had scored the winning goal in last season's FA Cup final. And he'd played in it!

Timothy Marley had never won anything with Westpool. Hadn't even got close. Yet he was still fondly remembered by Athletic fans old and young, simply because he had scored more goals for the club than anyone else.

Just two seasons earlier, Marley had been voted as the best player in Westpool's history, comfortably beating Jacob into second place. As a result, a statue of Marley had been erected outside the club's stadium.

Jacob hated that statue. He firmly believed that he was a far better player than Marley had ever been. He couldn't understand why the club's fans couldn't see it.

Well they would. Just as soon as he

broke Marley's goal scoring record.

As Jacob settled down in his expensive Italian leather settee and waited for the adverts to finish, he licked his lips as he thought about all the extra rewards that would come his way once he became Westpool's all-time leading scorer. There would be more sponsorship deals, increased offers to appear on talk shows or to be an occasional pundit on live football shows. The money would roll in even quicker than it did already.

It went without saying that he would also ask for a wage increase as well. Okay, so he was already the best paid player in the Premier League, but there were still players playing for European clubs who earned more than he did.

As Athletic's all-time leading scorer he could demand to earn at least as much as them.

And if Westpool refused to pay what he was worth... well, then he'd have to join another team that would.

The fans would understand, he assured himself.

The Christmas bonus

Predictably, as happened every single time Timothy Marley appeared on the sports news channel, the ex-footballer was asked to give his thoughts about Jacob.

Equally predictably, Marley answered the question in a polite and positive manner. He praised Westpool's current star striker and admitted it wouldn't be too long before Jacob broke his record.

"Although he hasn't scored a goal for three matches, so maybe the pressure's starting to get to him," the male presenter joked.

Marley smiled good-naturedly. "All strikers go through a drought at some point," he replied evenly. "I once went five games without scoring, so I'm sure he won't be too worried. Jacob Anderson is too good a player not to start scoring again soon."

"That's about the most sensible thing I've ever heard Marley say," Jacob muttered, as he watched the interview from the comfort of his comfy settee. "I'll be scoring goals again before you know it, innit."

"Especially now you've got your lucky blue pants all dried," Norris quipped, with more than a slight hint of bitterness in his voice.

"Shut up Norris. No one asked for your opinion," Jacob snapped irritably, without removing his eyes from the TV screen. "Haven't you got something useful that you could be doing? Like ironing my socks?"

Once again Norris fought down the urge to reply bad temperedly to Jacob's barbs. After all, it was time for him to be heading home for the day. Therefore, it was also finally time to find out what his Christmas bonus would be.

Norris gave a little cough to clear his throat. "Actually, it's time for me to be going," he responded. "It's gone five."

"Already? Well I suppose you better be off then. See-ya."

Norris didn't move.

It took a Jacob a few moments to realise that Norris was still in the room. It was only when his assistant made another quiet coughing noise that he became aware of the other man's presence.

For the first time since the TV had been switched on, the footballer turned his head so it was no longer facing the ginormous screen. He looked directly at Norris. "Are your legs okay?" he asked sarcastically. "I said see-ya. That means you can leave. Bye."

"Well..." Norris began. "It's just that... a little earlier you mentioned something about a... erm... Christmas bonus?"

"Oh so I did," said Jacob cheerfully. He turned away from Norris and once again fixed his gaze on the television. "Your Christmas bonus. How silly of me to forget."

Norris smiled. He wasn't sure why, but he had a feeling that Jacob was going to be extra generous this year.

He couldn't have been more wrong.

"You can have tomorrow off," said Jacob.

Norris smiled and waited patiently for his employer to finish his sentence. After a minute or so of silence, Jacob once again turned to face his assistant.

"Why are you still here?" the footballer asked.

"Because I'm still waiting to hear what my Christmas bonus is going to be," Norris replied.

"Do you need your ears cleaning out or something? I just told you what your Christmas bonus is. You can have tomorrow off."

Norris chuckled nervously – a reaction that only served to make the expression on Jacob's face turn from one of confusion to one of anger. "What now?" the footballer asked, sounding annoyed.

Suddenly Norris realised that Jacob wasn't actually joking.

His bonus really was that he would be getting the following day off. A day he was already due to have off. "But I wasn't supposed to be working tomorrow anyway," he whined. "It's Christmas Day. I never work on Christmas Day."

"And you won't be working on Christmas Day this year. I've just given you the day off. Now go home, enjoy a day with your family and I'll see you at 7am on Boxing Day. Don't be late. We've got a 12:45 kick-off and I'll need you to give the house a clean before you drive me to the stadium." With that Jacob turned his back on Norris to watch the television again.

Norris's face drained of all colour. He had never felt so angry in all his life. "But –"

"But nothing," said Jacob, interrupting his assistant. "There's no need to thank me. I really do insist that you have tomorrow off. Now get going before I change my mind."

"But—" Norris tried once again, only to be interrupted by his employer for a second time.

"Look, if you haven't left the room by the time I count to five then I'll change my mind and you won't get a bonus at all. One... two..."

Norris sadly shook his head and stomped miserably out the room slamming the door behind him.

Tears of anger were streaming down his face.

Marley's message

Jacob smiled as he stretched out on his settee and closed his eyes.

In spite of the fact he'd had to go through the inconvenience of attending football training that morning, he'd still had a more than enjoyable day.

Watching Norris parading up and down the high street whilst waving a pair of pants above his head had been good fun. The anguished expression on his assistant's face as he'd had to explain to the mother and her two sons why they couldn't have an autograph had been equally satisfying.

But the highlight of his day had undoubtedly been the look on Norris's face as it slowly dawned on him that he wouldn't be getting a Christmas bonus.

The footballer honestly couldn't understand why, just because it was Christmas, Norris should expect to receive anything other than his normal wage.

Just because he was a multi-multi-millionaire, other people were always expecting him to share his time and wealth with them.

Well, why should he? Jacob's view was that it was his talent and hard work – well, work – which had earned him that money, so it was his to do whatever he wanted with it.

And if others didn't like it? Tough!

He shuddered as he thought back to that Christmas eight years earlier when he had foolishly given his then agent one of his many cars.

What had he been thinking?

Jacob wriggled into an even more comfortable position on his soft leather sofa and could just feel himself starting to drift off to sleep when he suddenly heard a male voice clearly calling his name over and over again.

"Norris?" he called out, whilst slowly propping himself up onto his elbows.

The voice just continued calling Jacob's name.

"Norris? Is that you? Are you still here?"

Still the voice continued to call him.

Jacob sat up and shook his head violently from side to side.

Briefly, he worried that a burglar may have broken into his home. But then he decided that a burglar would be unlikely to go through the trouble of breaking into a home which featured every single state-of-the-art security system known to man, only to start calling for the person he was trying to rob.

Suddenly an even worse thought entered Jacob's head.

Maybe it was an autograph hunter!

The footballer stood up and edged himself quietly towards the corner of the room. He picked up a snooker cue that was leant against the wall. If there really was someone in his home then some kind of protection could well be needed.

Jacob gripped the snooker cue tightly and looked desperately around for his iphone. He couldn't see it anywhere. He wasn't used to having to look for things. Norris usually did that for him.

It was while he was frantically scanning the room for his iphone that he noticed something strange on the TV.

The sports news channel was still on and Timothy Marley was still being interviewed.

But the former Westpool striker was no longer looking and talking to the two presenters. Instead, it appeared to Jacob as though the man on the giant TV screen was looking directly at him. What's more, it looked like he was saying 'Jacob' over and over again.

The footballer rubbed his eyes. He was convinced he must have been seeing things.

He wasn't.

The very moment he stopped rubbing his eyes and stared at the screen, the man on the TV directly addressed him.

"Finally got your attention, have I?" Marley asked, following the question with a mischievous chuckle.

Jacob was too scared to speak. He just stood staring wide-eyed at his massive television, unable to quite believe what was happening.

His heart was beating so fast that he

felt as though it would burst out of his chest at any moment.

"What's the matter, Anderson? Scared?" All trace of the genial, pleasant tone that Marley usually spoke with had disappeared. It was replaced by a far more menacing sound.

Once again the footballer found himself unable to speak. Or even move. He was paralysed by fear.

Marley laughed wickedly. "Not so big and brave now are we, hey? Anyway you needn't be scared. Well, not of me anyway. I'm just here to give you a friendly warning."

Jacob felt his knees buckle. He was sure he was going to collapse. It took every ounce of the strength he had left to stagger towards his sofa, where he let himself fall backwards into the soft Italian leather. Not once did he remove his eyes from the TV screen.

"Comfy?" Marley asked. An unpleasant smirk spread across his usually friendly face. "Then I'll begin. This very night will be one of great unrest for you. You will be visited by three apparitions, each one of whom will present to you three visions of Christmas; one lived, one present and one yet to come. Take heed of what you see,

Anderson. If you don't the name Jacob
Anderson will mean nothing to anyone
in years to come. You'll be forgotten,
unloved and as poor as poor can be. Do
you understand?"

A shiver worked its way up Jacob's
back. His whole body was trembling,
and his bottom lip had started to wobble
uncontrollably. Marley laughed again,
gleefully. Then he fixed Jacob with a hard
and serious stare. "Do you understand,
Anderson?"

Jacob was just about to try and
nod when he suddenly stopped. The
expression on his face changed from one
of pure fear to one of total confusion.

"I... I... do have a question actually," he
mumbled.

"Go on."

"What's an apparition?"

Marley rolled his eyes and tutted loudly.
"Oh for goodness sake," he said, sounding
well and truly exasperated. "It really is
true what they say about some modern
footballers isn't it! An apparition is a
ghostly being. You'll be visited by three
ghosts tonight. Get it? Got it? Good."

"Ghosts?" Jacob wailed. "I don't want to
be visited by ghosts, I don't like ghosts.
Please Marley, I mean Timothy. Please

help me. Tell me this can be stopped. What do I have to do? Please. Tell me!"

Marley let out a burst of maniacal laughing. Jacob curled up into a ball on his sofa and pulled a cushion over his face whilst continuing to plead with the man on the TV for help.

Within seconds the laughing stopped.

Jacob pulled the cushion slowly away from his face and sneaked a quick glance at the TV. The face of Marley was gone, replaced instead by an advert for a tasteless fizzy drink that Jacob would never, ever drink himself. Not that this stopped him from being paid millions of pounds a year to be one of the brand's global faces.

"It was just a dream," Jacob said to himself, his heart rate returning to somewhere approaching its normal speed. He started laughing loudly. "It was all just a stupid dream."

His laughter didn't last long, though.

For seconds later he heard a strange sound.

A much treasured gift

There could be little doubt that in the years since he had first become a professional footballer, Jacob had bought a lot of stuff.

And while there was no way he could possibly account for all the tat that he had accumulated over the years, he was fairly certain that he had never at any time purchased a grandfather clock.

Yet, whilst sitting alone on his sofa, still slowly recovering from the unsettling experience he'd just had, Jacob was in no doubt that the strange sound he could now hear was the loud clang of a grandfather clock sounding the time.

It was a sound he remembered well from spending time at his grandparents' house in his youth. He hadn't liked the sound much then. It truly terrified him now.

Seven loud chimes came and went before silence filled the room. At first Jacob was simply relieved that the clanging had stopped, but he quickly realised that all was still not as it should be.

There was no sound coming from the television and Jacob was certain he hadn't turned the volume down. The picture had disappeared too.

"Great," Jacob muttered miserably to himself. "I'm having weird dreams, hearing strange noises and now my beautiful television is broken. It's just not fair!"

"Did you say something?" said a booming male voice from somewhere inside the room.

Jacob looked around frantically, unable to locate where the voice had come from.

"I'm over here. On the TV."

The footballer slowly peeked up at the screen. Sure enough, the picture had reappeared. Jacob found himself looking at a large, heavily bearded, middle-aged man sitting all alone in the sports news studio.

"I believe you've been expecting me," the man continued in a jovial manner, a friendly smile spreading across his round face. "I'm the Ghost of Christmas Past. Marley did tell you I was coming, didn't he? I do hate it when I surprise people. Which isn't the greatest personality trait for a ghost to have if I'm being totally honest."

A stunned expression fell across Jacob's face. "B... b... but that was just a dream. I was asleep. I must still be asleep. This can't be happening."

The Ghost of Christmas Past laughed heartily again. "You'd be surprised by how many people put ghostly appearances down to dreams. But no, I'm as real as real can be. There's no need to be worried, though, I'm just here to show you something. You just settle back into that lovely sofa of yours – and it really is a lovely sofa if you don't mind me saying – and keep your eyes on the TV, which is also pretty stunning by the way. Not many people I've visited get their visitations in this high definition, I can tell you. Oh you do have a lovely place here Mr Anderson. You've done well for yourself. Very well indeed. Anyway, where was I? Oh yes, that's right. Eyes on the screen and I'll see you in a little while."

At once the vision of the affable ghost disappeared from the screen. It was immediately replaced by the sight of two young boys standing in a snowy car park.

The boys were both aged around 11 or 12 years old. One had short, cropped brown hair, a handsome face and stood a good few inches taller than his friend.

As well as being short, the other boy was extremely skinny and had a scruffy mop of brown hair that would have completely covered his eyes, were it not for the fact that a rectangle shape had been cut into his fringe to allow him to see.

Watching from the comfort of his settee, an already astonished Jacob found himself even more amazed. "That's me and Norris from when we were kids, innit," he gasped, even though there was no one else in the room to hear him

Back on the television, the two boys looked nervous. "How much longer?" the taller boy asked, restlessly bouncing from one leg to the other.

"Any minute now, Jacob, just have patience" replied the other, looking at his watch.

Within seconds, a third person appeared on the screen. It was a man in his early 30s, dressed in a Westpool Athletic tracksuit. A woolly beanie hat was pulled tightly over his head.

"There he is," squealed the young Jacob excitedly, pointing at the man. "That's Timothy Marley."

For a moment, the boy just stood motionless, unable to do anything but point at the footballer, who was walking towards a blue BMW M5 that was parked in a corner of the car park.

"Well go and get his autograph then. That is why we've been standing here for the past two hours," laughed the 11-year-old Norris.

"I can't," whined Jacob. "I'm too nervous. What if he says no?"

"Why would he say no? It will only take him 30 seconds. And it's Christmas Eve. What sort of a heartless so-and-so would refuse a child an autograph on Christmas Eve? Look, come over with me and I'll ask him for you."

The two boys hurried over to where Timothy Marley was getting into his car. "Excuse me. Mr Marley?" Norris called out as he and Jacob ran quickly, but carefully, across the car park.

"Yes boys, what can I do for you?" replied Marley in a welcoming tone.

Norris waited for Jacob to say something. It soon became apparent, though, that Jacob was far too star-struck to be able to speak. "My friend Jacob here was wondering whether you'd sign this piece of paper for him. You're his favourite player."

The footballer took the scrap of paper and a biro pen from Norris and looked at it. A frown spread across his face, which up until that point had looked nothing but friendly.

"I'm not signing this," said Marley dismissively, handing the pen and paper back to Norris and climbing into his car.

Jacob looked utterly crestfallen. He turned away from Norris as he felt tears begin to sting the corner of his eyes. There was no way he wanted to let his best friend see him cry.

However, less than half a minute later Marley stepped back out of the car holding two brand new Westpool shirts and a special marker pen. "Here you go boys," he said leaning the shirts on the roof of his car so that he could sign them. "I'm sure you'd like these shirts signed better than that piece of scrap paper."

The two boys nodded, both rendered almost speechless by the footballer's generosity.

"Merry Christmas boys," said Marley cheerfully, before settling back into the BMW and driving off.

Back in his man den, the picture on Jacob's television disappeared again. Seconds later the Ghost of Christmas Past reappeared on the screen.

Reminiscing

As he had sat watching the episode from his past being replayed in front him, Jacob's facial expression had undergone many transformations.

At first he'd looked terrified. Then confused. Then amazed. Then, gradually, he had begun to smile as the memories of that long ago Christmas Eve came flooding back to him.

However, upon finding himself face-to-face with the ghost once again, he simply looked astonished.

The Ghost of Christmas Past smiled genially at the footballer. "Well, Mr Anderson. That must have been a thoroughly pleasant Christmas for you. What a fantastically generous gift to be given."

Jacob nodded. "I can't believe Marley did that," he said, a tone of pure bewilderment in his voice.

The ghost laughed again. "I know. Two brand new signed Westpool shirts without even being asked for them. As I said, a fantastically generous gift."

For a moment, Jacob looked confused. Then he blushed slightly. "Actually I meant I can't believe he lent on his car to sign the shirts. I mean, he could have scratched the paintwork, innit! But you're right, I suppose. Him giving me and Norris those shirts was a really nice thing to do."

"What did you do with that shirt, Mr Anderson, if you don't mind me asking?"

Jacob thought for a moment. "I got my Mum and Dad to get it framed for me," he recalled. "I hung it on my bedroom wall." The footballer smiled again as he reminisced. "I used to look at that shirt whenever I came home from school, or football training, or wherever and I'd promise myself that one day I'd wear a Westpool shirt for real. Then I could..." The footballer hesitated before finishing his sentence.

"Then you could what, Mr Anderson?" the large ghost asked, cordially.

"... Then I could make other people happy," Jacob added, guiltily.

"Oh that would be nice, wouldn't it, Mr Anderson? I'd love to be able to make other people happy. It must be far better than scaring them all the time. Still, I guess us ghosts don't really have much of a choice when it comes to that sort of thing, do we?"

Jacob let out a long sigh as he thought back to the way he had treated the mother and her two sons earlier that evening. But before he had a chance to say anything else to the Ghost of Christmas Past, he once again heard a clanging noise.

As the clangs became louder, the picture on the television screen began to flicker and the image of the big, friendly, bearded man began to fade away.

By the eighth clang the face of the first ghost had disappeared completely, only to be replaced by that of a stern-looking elderly lady, who Jacob couldn't help but think looked exactly like his old head teacher from secondary school.

"Oh no," moaned the woman on the television. "As if having to work on Christmas Eve every year wasn't bad enough already, this year I've got to spend it in the company of a complete dimwit."

Through the keyhole

It took Jacob a moment or two to realise that the woman on the TV was actually talking about him. Nobody had spoken to the footballer like that in years.

Not since he'd been at secondary school, in fact.

"Yes I mean you, Jacob Anderson," the woman continued. Her tone still surly. "Don't look so surprised. You should have known I was coming. I take it you do know who I am?"

Jacob frowned. "Are you Mrs Harris from Southdown Secondary School?"

"Oh don't be so stupid. You really are an utter dimwit aren't you!" the woman continued, her manner becoming increasingly aggressive. "I'm the Ghost of Christmas Present and I have to say I've got far better things that I could be doing tonight than talking to imbeciles like you."

"Hey, that's out of order. I'm worshipped by thousands of people throughout the country, innit. You can't talk to me like that," whined Jacob.

The Ghost of Christmas Present scowled at Jacob. It was a look designed to make it clear to the footballer that she didn't want any further interruptions. "Look, I don't want to be here, you don't want me here, so just shut up and watch the telly so that I can get going and do something more interesting. I'm sure there's some paint drying somewhere that I could be watching."

Before Jacob had a chance to say anything in response – not that he really wanted to – the ghost disappeared from the TV screen and the footballer soon found himself staring instead at a row of houses.

At first there didn't appear to be anything particularly special about the houses. They just looked like a normal row of semi-detached and terraced properties, similar to those found on streets in towns the length and breadth of the country.

They reminded Jacob of the very house he had grown up in as a child.

He afforded himself a quick look around his man cave and smiled smugly, He had certainly come a long way since those days.

Upon glancing back at the TV, the footballer noticed that the camera had started to pan down the street, showing him even more houses. Almost all of them were lit up by Christmas lights and although it didn't look to Jacob as though the owners of the houses could be particularly wealthy, most of the homes looked well cared for nevertheless.

However, one house stood out from the rest. It was this house that the camera eventually stopped and focussed on.

Unlike the other properties in the street, this house had no Christmas lights hanging from the exterior walls. The front lawn looked as though it hadn't been cut for months. The fence had panels missing. The windows were smeared to the point where Jacob doubted you could see through them, and the bottom section of the glass-panelled front door was boarded up.

Jacob shuddered. "You'd never catch me living in a house like that," he said aloud, unsure of whether the Ghost could still hear him or not.

Back on the TV screen, the camera began moving ever closer to the house's front door before moving ghostlike through it so that Jacob found himself looking at what he guessed must be the front room.

To Jacob's surprise, the front room was

clean and tidy and, in spite of the old
and tatty Christmas decorations that
were dotted around the room, it looked
perfectly cosy. If a little small and poky
for his own tastes.

It was then that he heard voices coming
from somewhere off screen.

"He really is a miserable, horrible little
so-and-so," said a woman's voice. "I was
really hoping that we'd be able to afford
to buy a lawnmower in the January
Sales, or pay someone to come in and fix
our front door or our fence... or just be
able to treat ourselves to something!"

"I know. I'm sorry love," said a male
voice. "I'll try and look for another
job in the New Year. But there really
doesn't seem to be anything around at
the moment. I've been looking, but I
don't seem to have the right skills or
experience needed for anything. I'm
definitely never going back there, though.
Not after today. No way!"

Jacob's mouth fell wide open. He
recognised that voice all too well, and
quickly realised that he must be somehow
spying on Norris's house.

The clock hanging on the wall of the
Sculley's front room showed that it
was just after 8pm. Jacob checked his

platinum Rolex watch to confirm that was indeed the time. It was.

Seconds later, Norris and his wife appeared on the screen carrying some wrapped Christmas presents which they placed under an artificial and sparsely decorated Christmas tree situated in the far corner of the room.

"I know you try love, and I know how hard you work," said Mrs Sculley affectionately to her husband. "At least we've managed to save up enough to get the kids the presents they wanted. So what if it means we have to live in a pig sty for a few more months. It'll be worth it when we see the looks on their faces tomorrow morning."

Tears started to well up in the corner of Mrs Sculley's eyes and her voice became croaky. "It just makes me so angry to think of that... that... wally sitting at home in his stupid mansion thinking he's better than everyone else just because he's so rich. He really is a nasty little..."

"Now, now dear," interjected Norris, before his wife could finish her sentence. "Don't upset yourself. After what's happened today I'm finished with him for good. I can't believe he used to be my best friend. For years I've defended him, certain that underneath all his meanness, deep down he was still the same person that I've known since I was five. Now I know he's evil, pure and simple. Don't waste your time thinking about him. I certainly won't anymore. I won't let him spoil our Christmas."

His wife attempted a smile, "But what will we do for money? Things are tight enough as it is."

"Don't worry about the money. Something will turn up I'm sure of it," said Norris as reassuringly as he could. "Anyway, there's more to life than money."

Norris pulled his wife close to him and gave her a big hug.

Back in Jacob's man den the picture on the television screen began to fade away and seconds later the footballer found himself once again faced by the unwelcome sight of the Ghost of Christmas Present.

Points of view

The ghost could tell from the look of anger on Jacob's face that the footballer was far from happy with what he had just watched.

"Did you enjoy the show?" the ghost asked, her voice full of scorn.

"Funnily enough, no I didn't," said Jacob gruffly. "If you must know I found it quite upsetting, innit."

"That was kind of the point you dimwit. And please stop saying 'innit'. It makes you sound even more stupid than you actually are, which admittedly is something that I wouldn't have thought was possible before I met you. So now how do you feel about the way you treat poor old Norris? Suitably bad I hope."

Immediately the expression on Jacob's face transformed from one of anger to total disbelief. "About the way I treat Norris!" he cried out, sounding genuinely appalled. "Why should I feel bad? I gave him a job when no one else would. If it wasn't for me his house would look in an even worse state than it does already! He should be thanking me. But instead he wants to leave to try and find a job somewhere else. Well good. Let him go. I don't need him anyway."

Jacob readied himself for a typically angry response from the ghost.

Instead, though, the Ghost of Christmas

Present just started cackling. It was a sound that unnerved the footballer even more than her previous abruptness had.

"You don't need him?" she said, in between bouts of uncontrollable, deranged-sounding, laughter. "Oh, that's a good one. I didn't expect you to be funny."

After a few more seconds of shrill laughter, the ghost fixed Jacob with a serious stare and her previous brusqueness quickly returned. "If, as you say, you really don't need him, then just who, exactly, is going to look after you? You've become so reliant on Norris that you can't even change the channel on the TV without him."

Jacob rolled his eyes. "Don't be silly. Of course I can. I'm not as much of an idiot as you like to make out."

"Is that so?" the ghost asked, raising an eyebrow inquisitively. "Do it then."

Jacob's eyes quickly flickered around the front room, desperately searching for the remote control. He couldn't see it anywhere.

"I'll do it later," he said, trying, but failing, to sound defiant. "Anyway, I can always hire someone else to do what Norris does. There are plenty of other people out there who could replace him."

"You really don't get it, do you?" the ghost continued. She suddenly sounded more sad than angry. "No one else would let themselves be humiliated the way you humiliate him. Not for what you pay anyway. The only reason he lets you get away with it is because for so many years you were best friends. Until today, he for some reason refused to see you for what you really are. A selfish, arrogant, bullying dimwit."

Jacob was just about to once again brush off what the ghost was saying, when suddenly her words started to sink in.

"But... what will he do without a job? He won't have any money. He needs me. Doesn't he?"

"Did you not listen to a word he just said? There's more to life than money. Like family and happiness. Maybe it's time you realised that."

Jacob slumped back onto his expensive sofa.

He suddenly felt winded; as though a football had been kicked full pelt into his stomach.

For as the TV screen went blank and he once again heard the eerie clangs of

the invisible grandfather clock begin
to strike, he finally started to realise
something.

He needed Norris far more than Norris
needed him.

The silent treatment

Have you ever been on a roundabout
or rollercoaster ride where you've been
spun so fast that when you get off you're
unable to walk straight or focus properly
on anything around you?

That's exactly how Jacob felt as he
sat on his sofa, trying to make sense of
everything that had happened to him
over the past few hours.

Since six o'clock, he had spoken to
Timothy Marley; been visited by two
ghosts; watched a happy moment from
his own past played out in front of him;
and gone on a clandestine visit to his
former best friend's home, all without
having to leave the supreme comfort of
his luxurious leather sofa.

So lost in thought was Jacob, as he
sat thinking about everything that he'd
just seen and heard, that he hadn't even

noticed that the grandfather clock had been silent since it had sounded its ninth chime quite a few minutes earlier.

He also hadn't noticed that the picture on the television screen had reappeared.

It took a few minutes for the footballer to look up and notice something that shocked him.

He was being watched.

He suppressed a scream at the vision on the television, quickly realising that this must be the third ghost Timothy Marley had warned him about.

This ghost, though, was quite unlike the previous two.

While the male ghost had looked, and indeed turned out to be, friendly and the female ghost had ended up being every bit as unpleasant as she'd originally appeared, there was simply no way for Jacob to be able to tell quite what this ghost would be like.

For the footballer merely found himself looking at the silhouette of a person. There was no way for him to tell if the person was male or female. It was as though he was looking at a shadow.

Yet, in spite of the fact he couldn't see a face, Jacob couldn't help but feel that the ghost was studying him intently. It was an extremely daunting, unsettling, sensation.

"W... w... what do you want from me, ghost?" Jacob just about managed to blurt out. The panic and fear that he was feeling was clearly audible in his voice.

The picture on the screen didn't move. No reply was forthcoming.

For a moment Jacob wondered if he'd accidentally managed to turn the volume down on the TV. Instinctively, he reached for the remote control in order to turn it back up again. Then he remembered that he didn't have a clue where the remote control was and instantly felt a pang of regret that Norris would no longer be around to help him solve such minor dilemmas.

"C... c... can you hear me?" the footballer called out, nervously.

Again, there was no movement or sound from the television. However, for some reason Jacob was certain that the silhouette could indeed hear him. He also got the impression that the image on the screen was very much enjoying his discomfort, although quite why he felt this he didn't know.

No matter what was happening, though, Jacob had never felt so terrified, or so alone, in all his life. "P... p... please say something, anything. I beg you."

For about 30 seconds nothing happened. Then, the silhouette slowly raised its right arm high in the air, held it there for a couple of seconds and then brought it down, quick as a flash.

Immediately the being on the TV disappeared and the screen once again went blank. Much to Jacob's obvious relief.

However, that relief turned to shock just a few seconds later, when the picture returned.

This is your life

Although he couldn't be 100 per cent certain, Jacob was pretty sure that the person now staring back at him from the television screen was none other than himself.

Not him as he looked at the moment. Modern-day Jacob certainly didn't have that many wrinkles – not with all the expensive face creams he used – and his hair was still very much on his head. The person on the television screen, meanwhile, was as bald as bald could be.

Yet there could be little doubt that in many other ways the person on the television looked just like Jacob. Albeit a much, much older version.

Sitting on his sofa, Jacob purposely began gently patting his face and touching his hair, just to make sure that all was as it should be.

It was.

"Thank goodness for that," he said to himself, breathing a huge sigh of relief.

"Jacob Anderson is Westpool Athletic's all-time leading goal scorer," said a voice from the television screen, as the picture continued to focus on the old man's face. *"Talented, good looking and rich, Jacob had it all,"* the voice continued.

Jacob smiled broadly to himself. This, he realised, must be a vision from the future.

He quickly figured out that he must be watching one of those television programmes that look back at the life of a sporting great. Jacob had watched a similar programme featuring Timothy Marley just last week and had wondered then if a similar programme would ever be made about him.

Here, it appeared, was his answer.

"Looks like I won then, Timmy," said Jacob, smugly, as for the first time in a good few hours he settled comfortably into his sofa and started to enjoy himself.

His enjoyment didn't last for long.

"And then he lost it all," said the voice on the screen, flatly.

Jacob's jaw fell wide open and his whole body started to tremble. "WHAT!" he screamed at the top of his voice, barely able to contain his rage. "HOW?"

The picture on the TV screen cut away from the elder Jacob and began showing some of the footballer's best goals for Westpool. Watching from his sofa, Jacob couldn't remember which goals he'd already scored and which he hadn't. They were all pretty good, though, even if he did think so himself.

The voiceover soon continued its narrative. *"Flash and arrogant, Anderson had long enjoyed the financial trappings that came with being a professional footballer. In addition to a mammoth country mansion, he also owned a fleet of vehicles that were the envy of even the most ardent car fanatics."*

The picture on the screen cut away from showing Jacob's goals to display an image of the mansion he was currently sitting in. As the camera panned up the driveway, Jacob was afforded a glimpse of his impressive array of cars. The collection included a red convertible Lamborghini, a blue Aston Martin DB9 Coupe and a silver Maserati Ghibli.

Despite his trepidation of what was about to occur, Jacob couldn't help but smile proudly as he watched his impressive collection of cars, including those he was yet to buy, paraded on the screen in front of him.

He really did love his cars.

"His problems started, though, just after he broke Westpool's goal scoring record, which had previously been held by Athletic legend Timothy Marley," the voiceover continued, as the images on screen went from showing Jacob's record breaking goal to some even more nostalgic shots of Marley in action.

"Demanding wages that would have doubled the highest earnings of any other player in the Premier League, Anderson was frozen out of the Westpool team and eventually sold to Spanish giants AFC Real Galacticos in a record breaking deal. It made Anderson the highest paid footballer on the planet."

As Jacob watched his future self

arrive by helicopter onto the pitch at the Galacticos' stadium to be greeted by thousands of ecstatic, cheering Real fans, he was at a complete loss to work out just what could possibly have gone so wrong. Everything was going exactly as he wanted it to.

"It was in Spain where things started to go wrong," stated the voiceover, as if seeking to provide Jacob with an answer. *"Anderson immediately angered the Real Galacticos' management team and his teammates by refusing to learn Spanish and insisting that everyone speak to him in English or not at all. A request that was ignored by everyone."*

On screen, footage of a Galacticos' training session clearly showed Jacob being isolated by his teammates and ignored by his manager.

"His performances on the pitch didn't help matters. He failed to score in his first six games, a failure which he publicly blamed entirely on his teammates for not passing to him at every available opportunity," the narrator continued.

Jacob watched, horrified, as on screen he saw himself miss numerous easy goal scoring opportunities.

"Within two months of arriving in Spain

*amid much fanfare, Jacob Anderson
found himself dropped from the team.
It was then that he reverted to doing
the one thing he knew he was still good
at. Spending money. However, if his
purchases in England were thought
to be excessive, in Spain his spending
became totally out of control. More luxury
cars were purchased, as was a nine-
bedroom villa complete with two tennis
courts, three outdoor swimming pools
and a heli-pad. It was when he bought a
helicopter, though, that it became obvious
to many that Jacob Anderson had serious
problems."*

Back on his sofa, Jacob couldn't
understand what the narrator could
possibly be talking about. From what
he could see of the house, the cars and
the helicopter, he owned the kind of
belongings that most people could only
dream of owning.

So what if he wasn't getting in the team!
Jacob couldn't care less about his football
career. Not if he was going to become as
rich as it appeared he was.

Again, it didn't take the voiceover
man on the television long to provide
Jacob with some more answers. *"As
Anderson continued to show more*

*interest in spending money than he did
playing football, many of his lucrative
sponsorship deals began to dry up.
While his wages remained sky high, the
sponsorship money and appearance, win
and goal bonuses which had previously
funded his extravagant lifestyle,
disappeared. By the end of his first season
in Spain Jacob found himself in severe
debt. Even the sale of his beloved cars,
houses and helicopter left the footballer
teetering on the edge of bankruptcy."*

Jacob shifted uncomfortably in his seat.
The thought of being without money
scared him more than anything he could
imagine.

Even more than the silhouette ghost.

Or so he thought.

*"However, it was during the close season
that Jacob Anderson's world really came
tumbling down,"* the narrator continued,
ominously. *"The tragic death of his one-
time agent and former best friend Norris
Sculley in a car crash came as a huge
shock to him..."*

"No! Not Norris! Please not Norris,"
Jacob screamed at the television. His
hands involuntarily covered his eyes as
the programme displayed the wreckage of
a Porsche Cayenne – the very one Jacob

had given his then friend many years earlier.

"... *But when Jacob found himself blamed in the press by Norris's estranged wife for ruining her late husband's life, the footballer found himself being hounded day and night by journalists. He was even branded by one paper as being 'Britain's biggest bully'."*

"NO MORE, PLEASE," Jacob yelled again. "Please make this stop, I'm sorry. I'm so very, very sorry." Tears were streaming down his face as he slumped from his sofa onto his knees.

The last image that Jacob saw before the screen finally went blank, was a photo of Norris, along with his wife and three children, unwrapping Christmas presents in the front room of their house. They were the very same presents that Jacob had seen the elder Sculleys carry into their front room earlier that evening.

Jacob let out another angered scream, before the silhouette ghost once again appeared on the TV in front of him.

Questions without answers

If you'd have asked Jacob just a few minutes earlier whether he ever wanted to see the silhouette ghost again, his answer would have been a resounding 'no way'.

However, upon once again finding himself looking upon the strange shadowed being, the simple truth was that he couldn't have felt any more relieved.

Anything was better than what he'd just witnessed.

"Please tell me that what I've just seen doesn't have to happen?" Jacob wailed, desperately hoping the ghost would break its long silence.

It didn't.

"Is there anything I can do? Anything at all? Please! I beg you ghost. Just tell me that there's something I can do to stop all this from coming true. I really will do anything!"

The ghost remained motionless and silent. As before, though, it felt to Jacob as though the faceless being was somehow staring intently at him.

It was a hugely disturbing feeling.

"What do you want from me?" Jacob continued, his voice becoming ever more pleading. "Why have you shown me all these visions tonight?"

By now, Jacob was sobbing uncontrollably. Yet no matter how upset he got or how desperately he pleaded with the ghost for answers, the being on the TV didn't budge once.

Eventually, Jacob managed to summon up enough energy to rise from his knees. Once on his feet, he staggered unsteadily to the television. At first he tried turning the TV off in a desperate bid to get rid of the silent, shadowy ghost. It didn't work.

He then went to the back of the TV and pulled out the power lead.

When he went back to check the screen, though, he was horrified to find the ghost was still there.

Defeated, Jacob once again slumped to his knees. "I will change, I promise," he screamed at the television. He felt as though every last ounce of energy was being drained from his body. "From now on I'll be nice to Norris. I'll sign autographs for fans. I'll even sell some of my cars if I have to. I'll do anything it takes to stop what I've just seen from

coming true. Just tell me it's enough.
Please!"

Still there was no sound or movement
from the being on the TV screen.

Feeling well and truly exhausted, Jacob
rolled up into a ball on the floor and
began to rock himself gently to and fro.

After what felt like only a few minutes,
but in actuality must have been far
longer, he was suddenly startled from his
position on the floor by a sound from the
television.

*"Good morning and Merry Christmas to
you all,"* said one of the seemingly many
identical attractive female presenters on
the Sports news channel. *"Here's hoping
that you're waking up this morning to all
the presents from Santa that you were
hoping for."*

Jacob rubbed at his red, puffy eyes. He
looked towards one of the huge windows
at the far end of his man den and could
see that it was light outside. A quick
glance at his platinum Rolex watch
confirmed that it was already past 8
o'clock in the morning. Suddenly a huge,
relieved smile spread across his face.

"It really was all just a dream," he
reasoned aloud. The footballer began
laughing hysterically, while at the same

time berating himself for being so foolish as to believe he'd really been visited by ghosts during the night.

Pulling himself on to his sofa, he decided that he would relax for a bit in front of the television before going to make himself some breakfast.

It was only then that he realised the strange events of the previous night must have actually happened.

For as the face of Timothy Marley once again appeared on the screen, Jacob noticed that the TV's power lead was still unplugged!

The last thing Jacob saw as he rose from his feet and rushed out of the room was Marley winking at him.

Making amends – 1

The footballer hurriedly grabbed the nearest warm-looking coat he could find and forced on what he assumed were probably an extremely expensive pair of trainers. He didn't have a clue how much they would have actually cost in the shops. Despite being incredibly rich, most of his sponsors were only too happy to give him brand new clothes and accessories for free.

"Not anymore," Jacob stated to himself, as he rushed out of his front door and slammed it shut behind him.

Snow had just started to fall as Jacob emerged into the cold Christmas morning air. For a moment he considered going back into the house to grab a hat and some gloves, or maybe even phone for a taxi, but then he decided that he wanted to get to his destination as quickly as possible. Doing any of those things would only slow him up.

He doubted he'd be able to find his phone to call a taxi anyway. Even if he did he wouldn't have had a clue what number to call. He'd never used a taxi before in his adult life. Norris always drove him everywhere he needed to go.

Jacob sprinted down his driveway as fast as he could, taking as much care as possible not to slip over on the icy ground. As he ran past his hugely expensive fleet of cars he was sorely tempted to just jump in one and drive to where he was going. But he was already banned from driving and knew it would only make matters worse if he was pulled over by the police.

It's not like he wasn't well known, after all.

After about two minutes of running pretty much flat out, Jacob's pace slowed to a more gentile, yet still fairly fast, pace. Although he may not have enjoyed football training that much, especially the fitness sessions, Jacob had always been blessed with a naturally high level of fitness. Therefore, brisk early morning runs didn't bother him that much. Not that he could remember the last time he'd done one.

It took Jacob about half-an-hour to reach the edge of the town where Norris lived, during which time the snow had started to settle.

Although he had never been to his assistant's house before, Norris still lived in the town where both he and Jacob had grown up, so the footballer had a fairly good idea of where he was going.

He was just approaching the corner of Norris's road when he saw some people he recognised standing by a bus stop.

It was the mother and two sons who had been waiting outside his house the previous afternoon.

Desperate to avoid them, Jacob was just about to turn around and find another way to Norris's house, when he stopped. Instead of trying to avoid his fans, as he would usually have done, he instead marched purposely over to them.

"Hello boys. Happy Christmas," he said in his friendliest tone.

"Who's this and how do you know my sons?"asked the mother, a trace of suspicion clearly audible in her voice.

"Mum, shut up will ya," said one of the identical looking boys. "It's Jacob Anderson," he added, sounding well and truly star-struck.

"Oh," replied the woman, stiffly. "Well, I suppose he looks more like a footballer than that other chap who we spoke to yesterday. Are you sure you're allowed to speak to us now? You shouldn't be sleeping or anything?" She didn't even bother to try and hide the sarcasm from her voice.

Jacob's cheeks burned red at the memory of how appallingly he'd behaved a day earlier. "Yes. I'm truly sorry about that," he said. "It was an awful way for me to behave, but–"

"It certainly was," the woman interrupted before Jacob had a chance to finish his sentence. "We had to walk for hours from this town to your house.

Then we stood around waiting for you for ages in the freezing cold. Only for you to completely ignore us when you turned up. By the time we got back here we missed our bus home and now I find out that there's no service running on Christmas Day. Goodness knows what we'll do now. I don't have any more money to stay another night in a bed and breakfast."

"Mum, shut up will ya," said her other son. "You're embarrassing us in front of Mr Jacob."

"No, your mum's right," stated Jacob. "It was out of order the way I behaved yesterday." He really did feel truly terrible. He had no idea his behaviour could affect other people so negatively. Just then, a thought occurred to him. "I'd like to make it up to you. Can you just wait here for ten minutes? I promise I'll be back."

"Well..." the mother pondered... "It's not like we've got anywhere else to be. But if you're not back in ten minutes then–"

This time it was Jacob's turn to interrupt her. "I will be back, I promise," he said, flashing her his most affable smile. Without another word he turned and sprinted at full pelt the rest of the way to Norris's house.

Making amends – 2

At first Norris couldn't believe his eyes when he opened the front door only to find himself standing face to face with Jacob. Then, a look of pure panic swept across his face.

"There's no way I'm coming into work today. No way at all," he stated vehemently without so much as wishing his former friend and employer a Merry Christmas. "You gave me the day off and anyway I'm–"

"Quitting," laughed Jacob merrily, finishing Norris's sentence for him. "Yes, I'd heard that."

For a moment Norris looked confused, but before he had a chance to say anything further his wife joined him on the doorstep. Jacob shuddered as he noticed that both Norris and his wife were wearing the exact same outfits that he'd seen them wearing in the photo displayed on his television the previous evening.

"What does he want," Mrs Sculley asked angrily, barely affording Jacob more than a passing glance. "If he's come round to get you to come into work today then he can just forget it. Have you told him yet Norris? Have you?"

Jacob once again chuckled heartily. "Look, I understand why you may not like me. After all, the way I've treated Norris over the past few years has been nothing more than shameful. But... and I can't explain why... I'm a changed man. I promise you things are going to change. The Jacob you knew is no more. Or to put it more accurately, the Jacob you once knew, the one from when we were children, is back."

"Why should we believe you?" snapped Mrs Sculley, once again speaking before her husband had a chance to say anything.

"I'll have to prove it to you, I know that," replied Jacob earnestly. "But if you come back and work for me," he continued, turning to face Norris, "then I want you to become my financial adviser. I want you to take complete control of my money, and stop me from having my ludicrous spending sprees. I want you to help make me a better person. I want you to make sure I give money to charity and just do more good with the huge amounts that I earn. You'll get a pay rise, too, of course."

Although Jacob could tell that Norris and his wife were both hugely sceptical about what he was proposing, the footballer was delighted when, after a few minutes deliberation, Norris finally agreed to the offer.

"There's just one more thing," Jacob asked sheepishly. "Would it be possible to give me a lift back home?"

New beginnings

Jacob couldn't remember the last time he'd been happy. Not truly happy.

Sure, he loved his money, his expensive cars, his massive television, his country mansion and all his various other over zealously priced possessions. But as he sat down for his Christmas dinner later that afternoon, he realised that none of them had ever made him feel as happy as he did at that very moment.

For as he began carving the turkey – which it has to be said was probably larger than any turkey you're ever likely to see in your lifetime – he looked at the pleasure expressed on all the faces of the people around him.

Sitting at the table with him were Norris, his wife and their three children, along with the mother and her two young sons whom he'd spoken to at the bus stop.

Although Norris had initially refused Jacob's request to drive him back to his house, fearing that despite Jacob's promises he was still just looking for a personal slave, once the footballer had explained to him why he wanted a lift, Norris had been only too happy to agree to the appeal.

The two men had then driven to the bus stop where Jacob had personally asked the mother and her boys to join him for Christmas lunch.

If she hadn't been sure whether or not to accept the proposal at first, Jacob's further offer for them to stay the night at his house and then go and watch the following day's Westpool Athletic game as his personal guests, soon swayed her to accept.

Jacob had then asked Norris, along with his family, to join them, an offer which Norris had politely refused until he saw the size of the turkey on offer.

It was while he was tucking into his fourth roast potato that Jacob had another idea.

"How are you finding the old Porsche to drive?" he asked Norris.

For a moment his soon-to-be new financial adviser was taken a little aback. "It's... fine. I really like driving it," he said, not really sure why Jacob was asking him.

"Would you like to be driving something else more, though? Maybe an Audi R8? Maybe a Benz? A Range Rover? Well, take a look outside. Take your pick. Take all of them. It's not like I can drive them anyway, is it?"

So amazed was Norris by what Jacob was offering that he involuntarily spat out the mouthful of food that he'd been chewing. Bits of chewed up turkey and sprouts flew across the table, narrowly avoiding some of the other guests.

"There's just one thing, though," continued Jacob, as Norris apologised to all those he'd almost just deposited food over. "You have to let me take the Cayenne back so I can get it scrapped. Let me do that, and you can take any of the cars you want. I'll even pay your insurance for you."

Although Norris had no idea why Jacob was so insistent about getting a perfectly good car turned into scrap metal, there was no way he was going to argue about it. He'd got a real taste for some of those cars from driving Jacob here, there and everywhere over the years.

A little later that afternoon, while the Sculley children and the other two boys were, at Jacob's request, going through his collection of football shirts to see which ones they wanted to keep, and Mrs Sculley and the other boys' mother were relaxing in one of the houses' many living rooms, Jacob and Norris found themselves alone in the man den.

Both men were sitting on the luxury leather sofa in silence. Jacob wanted to apologise to Norris yet again for the way he'd behaved over the past few years, but he didn't know what more he could say.

Eventually, more to break the silence than anything else, he decided to go and switch the television on – remembering to plug the power lead back in first.

Seconds later, the Sports news channel was back on, and the first face that Jacob saw was none other than Timothy Marley. The channel was replaying the same interview that he had watched the previous evening.

"I suppose you want me to turn it over," joked Norris.

Jacob laughed. "No that's okay. I'm sure I can manage to do it myself. Well, actually, I could if only I could find that blooming remote control."

"I may be able to help you there," said Norris, a smile spreading across his face as he held out the missing remote. "I realised last night when I got home that I still had it in my hand when I stormed off. Sorry about that. I was going to drop it through your door at some point. Probably. Hope you didn't miss it too much."

Jacob stared at the remote control in Norris's hand and then looked at Norris and burst out laughing.

"What's so funny?" asked Norris, sounding perplexed.

"Nothing at all," replied the footballer, happily. "Merry Christmas Norris, old friend."

Jacob took the remote control from Norris's hand and began pressing buttons to bring up a new channel.

Although he would never be entirely sure, just before the TV switched from the sports news channel to the classic football match channel, Jacob could have sworn that, from inside the TV screen, Marley gave him a double thumbs up.

"Merry Christmas, Marley," said Jacob under his breath. "Merry Christmas everybody."